W9-BNL-161

THE LAST FRONTIER

ANTARCTICA

by Geoffrey T. Williams

Illustrated by Neesa Becker

PRICE STERN SLOAN

Los Angeles

The author wishes to thank
Dr. Paul K. Dayton and Dr. Mark Huntley,
Scripps Institute of Oceanography,
for their valuable time and assistance
in technical editing.

Library of Congress Cataloging-in-Publication Data

Williams, Geoffrey T.
Antarctica : the last frontier/by Geoffrey Williams;
illustrations by Neesa Becker
p. cm.
Summary: Jon accompanies his scientist mother to Antarctica, where he observes the animals and many wonders of that continent.
ISBN 0-8431-2995-6
[1. Antarctic regions—Fiction.] I. Title.
PZ7.W65915An 1992
[Fic]—dc20 91-29771
CIP
AC

Published by Price Stern Sloan, Inc.
11150 Olympic Boulevard, Suite 650, Los Angeles, California 90064

10 9 8 7 6 5 4 3 2 1
First Printing

ISBN: 0-8431-3378-3

ISBN: 0-8431-2995-6 (book and cassette)

Note to readers:

Like many explorers before him, Jon Michaels kept a journal of his extraordinary travels in Antarctica. In it he recorded the location of each event in longitude and latitude so that he could easily look it up on a world map or globe when he got home. You can follow his adventures by doing the same thing. He also gives the time using a "twenty-four-hour clock." 01:00 hours is one o'clock in the morning, 12:00 hours is noon, 24:00 hours is midnight. In a land where the sun can shine brightly almost twenty-four hours a day during the summer months, Jon found that this was the easiest way to remember when it was time to go to sleep!

October 8
55 degrees, 28 minutes west, 57 degrees south. Drake Passage. 19:00 hours. Temperature: -14°F. Wind speed: 80 mph. The storm is incredible! It's like being in a washing machine stuck on the heavy-duty cycle.

The freezing wind thundered up from the south, turning the ocean into a swirling, white-capped confusion. Towering waves hammered the deck like explosions and tossed the *Windhover* like a stick-boat in a storm drain.

Safe inside the ship's bridge, Jon Michaels held onto the railing, fighting to keep his balance, and fighting a growing case of sea sickness.

"Do you think MURV is okay?" his mother, Dr. Dorothea Michaels, shouted over the shrieking wind. MURV, the three-man research submarine operated by the Mid-Ocean Institute, was tied to the deck taking a tremendous pounding from the storm.

Captain Thorn peered through the streaked windshield. "Looks okay. She's strapped down pretty good."

"Is the weather always this bad?" Jon yelled.

"During the winter it can get a lot worse. This is just a spring breeze!" Captain Thorn yelled back.

Jon laughed. A spring breeze! In early October! Sure, seasons are turned on their heads in the bottom half of the world—July is the beginning of winter, and January, the start of summer—so it should be warm now, right? He checked the thermometer again. -18°F!

The ship was nose-down in a trough as another wave slammed into them. The bow all but disappeared under tons of water. Slowly, straining at every rivet, the sturdy ship righted itself, only to plunge into the next trough.

"The ocean around Antarctica is the roughest in the world," Jon's mother said.

"I believe it! But why is it so rough?"

"Antarctica's the world's biggest weather factory," she answered, bracing herself for the next wave.

"Weather factory? What do you mean?"

"First of all, Antarctica's the coldest, windiest place on earth—"

"How cold does it get?"

"Winter at the South Pole averages around -70°F. The coldest temperature ever recorded was almost -128°F. And wind speeds of 200 miles per hour have been measured—"

"That's stronger than a hurricane!"

"Well, don't worry. It's a lot nicer this time of year."

Jon was almost afraid to ask. "Uh, just how nice does it get?"

Captain Thorn answered, "Satellite weather reports say it'll be pretty toasty by the time we get to Palmer Station—25°F." Toasty? Well, anything would be better than this.

"Anyway," Dr. Michaels said, "freezing winds blow across Antarctica's ice cap all year long, making these big storms. Antarctica's weather affects the whole world."

The ship lurched violently as another wave hit. To Jon, the only thing Antarctica's weather was affecting was his stomach. Holding a hand over his mouth, he quickly made his way back down to his cabin.

October 11
61 degrees, 30 minutes west, 60 degrees
10 minutes south. South Shetland Islands.
0600 hours. Temperature: 5°F. Wind speed: 0
It's almost like being on another planet.
Stranger than anything I ever imagined.

The ocean was frozen. The air was still and cold. A distant fog blurred the horizon. It was hard to tell where the ocean stopped and the sky started. The *Windhover*, covered with a thick layer of frost, was a ghostly white.

They were on a ghost ship sailing a frozen sea.

Sheets of ice, three and four feet high and broad as parking lots, lifted and tilted on the rolling swells. The ship was plowing its way through, leaving a trail of dark, open water in its wake. "This is pack ice," Dr. Michaels said. "During the winter the sea freezes for hundreds of miles around Antarctica. Last night's storm—and the warmer weather—is helping to break it up."

A chorus of loud barking came from the other side of the ship. Jon and his mother hurried across and looked over the edge. Dozens of large, sleek seals were jumping on and off the pack ice near the ship. "Crabeater seals. And look! See the pups?" Dr. Michaels pointed at several babies.

"What are they doing?"

"Hunting for krill."

"What's krill?"

"Their food. Tiny crustaceans. Like shrimp. There are billions of them in the Antarctic ocean."

"How can seals live in freezing water?"

"They have several inches of fat under their skin that keeps them warm. It also helps them float, and it fills out their shape so they can swim fast. It's one reason so many were slaughtered."

"Slaughtered?" Jon couldn't imagine these graceful creatures being killed for anything. "Why?"

"For their fur and blubber. Seal and whale hunters were the first people to come to the Antarctic. And back in the early 1800s, British and American sealers killed and butchered millions of fur seals, elephant seals and whales. Coats made of seal fur used to be popular. And whale and seal blubber had a number of uses. Now there are laws that protect them, but it may be too late for some...."

"I know some kinds of whales are close to extinction," Jon said.

His mother nodded. "Humpback whales, bow whales, even the mighty blue whales. Scientists estimate there are less than 6,000 blue whales left."

Jon and his mother had swum and dived in many of the world's oceans, and always the whales had been welcome companions. He'd listened to the strange and wonderful songs of the humpbacks many times, wondering just what the marvelous creatures were singing about. And although he'd never seen a blue whale, the thought of the biggest animal that ever lived, larger even than the largest dinosaurs, being hunted to extinction, was painful.

Spotting a large shape in the distance ahead, he shaded his eyes to see better. "Is that a mountain?"

"It's a mountain all right," Dr. Michaels said. "Of ice."

"An iceberg?"

"It's called a tabular iceberg. Because it's flat on top, like a table."

It was a hundred feet tall, four miles long and a brilliant blue-white in color. Jon watched the massive shape as the ship drew nearer. "It's huge. Is it frozen seawater like the pack ice?"

"No. It's fresh water. Frozen snow and ice. Broken off from one of Antarctica's ice shelves or glaciers. But this one's not too big. A few years ago there was one more than ninety miles long—as big as the state of Connecticut—and 130 feet high. Of course, most of an iceberg is under the water. So it's actually about four times deeper than what you see."

"And Antarctica is covered by ice that thick?"

"Almost all of it. More than 90 percent of all the ice in the world is in Antarctica. Plus, there's as much freshwater in Antarctica's ice as in all the world's rivers and lakes."

The colossal floating sculpture glided by. The wind and waves had hollowed out fantastic shapes: caves and tunnels near the base, sharp-edged curves, glistening mirrored faces, jagged edges, fins, knife-points....

Jon noticed one steep edge had been scooped out, leaving a shelf of ice five or six feet above the water. Incredibly, as he watched, black-and-white bullet-shapes began popping out of the water and landing on the shelf one after the other. "Penguins!" he shouted.

"Those are chinstrap penguins."

"I'll bet they're called that because of the black band under their chin. Will we see more?"

"There are millions of penguins in Antarctica. Emperors, Adelies, chinstraps, gentoos. I imagine we'll see some of their rookeries later on."

"What's a rookery?"

"The places where they breed and raise their young. Some rookeries have more than a million penguins....Well, I need to see how MURV weathered the storm. You grab some breakfast. We'll be at Deception Island this afternoon, and we can do some swimming." She walked forward to where the little yellow sub was tied down, leaving Jon to look after her curiously.

The iceberg drifted by like a shining ice palace. The *Windhover* was surrounded by pack ice as far as the eye could see. Swim! Jon laughed. What a joke.

October 12
61 degrees, 30 minutes west, 62 degrees
50 minutes south. Deception Island.
21:00 hours. Temperature: 27°F.
Wind speed: 5 mph. Can you believe I'm
going to go swimming in a volcano?

The *Windhover* was anchored in the lagoon, which had been formed when the crater of Deception Island volcano collapsed and sunk. Jon and his mother were circling the lagoon in an inflatable boat. Almost two thousand feet overhead was the snow-capped peak of the island. Large birds—Antarctic terns—wheeled and cried in the air, their white wings glistening like bright sparks of fire.

Dr. Michaels pointed out the ruins of a Norwegian whaling station built in the early last century, a grim reminder of the time when whales were hunted and killed by the thousands.

Farther down the shore, Jon saw a jumble of fire-blackened buildings. "What happened there?"

"The volcano happened. That's what's left of a Chilean scientific station. Chile, Argentina and Great Britain had outposts here. But when the volcano erupted in 1967, everyone was forced to leave."

A few minutes later, she nosed the boat up onto the beach at Fumarole Bay and shut the engine off. The coarse lava and cinder rocks crunched underfoot as they stepped out. Moss grew in long green strips next to steaming cracks. Parts of the beach were too hot to walk on. The water, heated by the same underground volcanic activity, was almost 100°F. Before long, they were waist deep in water as warm as a hot tub.

Two large ships were making their way through the harbor entrance. The decks were lined with curious passengers. "I didn't know they had tour boats to Antarctica," Jon said to his mother.

"Chile and Argentina started tours in the late 1950s. Many countries have them now. They're very controversial."

"Why?"

"Some people think when tourists see Antarctica they'll understand how important it is to keep it clean and natural, and what a unique place it is for scientific research. Others think Antarctica should be left untouched by man. They're afraid tourists will interfere with the environment, disturb penguin and seal breeding grounds and leave litter behind. The more people who come here, the more chance there is for environmental damage. There's already been an oil spill from a ship that ran aground near Palmer Station. It polluted the water and killed wildlife."

Jon watched as the ships anchored and began lowering boats. Dozens of passengers climbed aboard, eager for their chance to swim in the volcano. Jon didn't know who was right about the tourists. He just knew he wouldn't have wanted to miss his chance.

October 14
64 degrees west, 64 degrees 30 minutes south. Anvers Island, Palmer Station. 22:00 hours. Temperature: 20°F. Wind speed: 5 mph. The cheeseburgers are great, the scientists are pretty cool and the hot tub is neat, but you can have the skuas. And those elephant seals...

"Don't forget your skua stick," Dr. Michaels said.

"My what?"

She handed him a long ski pole. "Just in case. Skuas build their nests all over the place, and if you get too near, they get mad. Watch out for their claws and their—" She gave him an odd grin. "Sometimes they dive-bomb people with, uh, you know."

"You mean like—pigeon poop?"

"Exactly! And their aim is very accurate."

"I'll be careful," Jon said, laughing. He left the mess hall and walked past the dormitory building, deciding to hike the short distance to the foot of the glacier behind the station.

He never made it that far.

Even though he was being careful, he must have stepped too near a nest. Suddenly he heard a loud flapping of wings and angry screeching. He looked up just in time to duck as a large bird dived at his head. Then the air seemed filled with screaming birds and flapping wings as half a dozen outraged skuas descended on him.

After keeping them back with his skua stick and dodging their messy droppings, Jon decided he could wait to see the glacier another day. But what began as an orderly retreat rapidly turned into a headlong run, with skuas dive-bombing him until he was finally out of their territory.

A few minutes later, breathing easier, he was standing on some rocks near the beach looking out across the waters of Arthur Harbor. The midnight sky was streaked with clouds. Soon the sun would dip below the horizon and Antarctica would know a brief twilight.

Less than a mile away lay several small islands: Torgersen, Litchfield, Humble—mountains of ice and rock jutting out of the dark water. There was a soft yellow glow to their snow-covered peaks—light did strange and beautiful things in Antarctica. Many miles to the south he could just make out the Transantarctic Mountains on the peninsula. Across the harbor a glacier spilled down from the island's mountainous interior, ending in sheer ice cliffs that plunged several hundred feet into the water.

On the rocky shore a dozen elephant seals were lazing the last hours of sunlight away, their round, brown bodies lumped together like loaves of bread dough. A beachmaster and his small harem of females. The beachmaster was almost fifteen feet long. Jon knew these huge mammals could weigh more than 8,000 pounds.

He edged a little closer.

The beachmaster slowly lifted his huge head and turned his liquid brown eyes on the boy. When he opened his mouth, stained, worn teeth gleamed dully in the light. He puffed up the loose sack of skin that hung over his nose like a small trunk, the source of his odd name, and let loose a deafening bellow. A ringing challenge to the intruder and, at the same time, a warning to the other seals.

Jon staggered back, almost tripping. Not because of the noise, and not because he was frightened, though he was, a little, but because the odor of fish was so incredibly, unforgettably, nauseatingly powerful. The stench of the seal's breath washed over him like a thick wave. He squeezed his eyes shut, then opened them, blinking away tears, and decided to observe the mammoth creatures from a more respectable distance.

In the water next to the Windhover. It's hard writing when you're bobbing up and down like a cork! It'll be better a couple of hundred feet down. This water is so cold you wouldn't live more than a few minutes in it if something went wrong. I sure hope MURV checks out okay. . . .

"Robot manipulators?" Captain Thorn asked, running through the checklist before taking MURV down.

"Check," Dr. Michaels answered.

"Video output?"

"Check."

"Detach mooring cable," Captain Thorn said.

Dr. Michaels flipped a switch and there was a muffled thump. "Mooring cable detached." The motors hummed quietly and MURV dropped beneath the freezing waters off the Antarctic Peninsula.

Captain Thorn switched on MURV's outside running lights. They lit up the water for twenty or thirty feet. Beyond the cone of light, the water was black as night. In the small cabin the only lights came from the glow of the instrument panels and video screens, the only sounds were the electric motors and the soft pinging of the sonar unit. "What are we looking for?" Jon asked.

"Krill." Dr. Michaels said while studying a radar screen.

"Why?"

"Because they're one of the most important parts of the food chain in the Antarctic Ocean."

"What's a 'food chain'?"

"It's a way scientists describe what eats what. Small animals get eaten by bigger animals, bigger animals get eaten by even larger animals, and so on. Down here it all starts with microscopic organisms called diatoms. The krill eat the diatoms—"

"And whales and seals and penguins eat the krill," Jon finished.

"One of the things I'm researching is how the krill are being affected by the depletion of the ozone in the earth's atmosphere."

"We've been studying the ozone layer in school. How man-made chemicals in the air are breaking it down."

"Do you know why it's important?"

"It has something to do with sunlight and radiation."

"Ultraviolet radiation is part of sunlight. The ozone layer filters out most of it. When too much reaches the earth, it can be harmful. Some scientists think it can cause cancer and cause the earth to get warmer."

"The greenhouse effect. We studied that, too."

"Right. And if the earth gets too warm, the ice caps could start melting, causing the oceans around the world to rise, which would cause flooding. A lot of the things we know about the ozone layer were discovered at the South Pole research station—" She was interrupted when the pinging of the sonar suddenly became louder and faster.

"There's something big out there," Captain Thorn announced.

"A school of krill," Dr. Michaels said. "And a huge one."

"We're heading right into the middle of it," the Captain said. "I'm going to stop." He turned off MURV's engines and the sub drifted to a standstill.

"I don't see anything," Jon said.

His mother smiled. "You will. Just watch."

A few tiny creatures swam by the bubble window. Then a few more. And more. Moments later there seemed to be hundreds. Then thousands. Then millions. A solid wall of squirming, wriggling, writhing krill blocked the window.

"Activate the external microphones," Dr. Michaels said.

Captain Thorn threw a switch and the cabin was flooded with a wash of sound. Clicking, snapping, popping. Like countless tiny radios giving off nothing but static. "I've got a reading on the size of the school," he said.

"How big?" Dr. Michaels was hurriedly taking notes.

He studied MURV's radar screens. "About one hundred and fifty yards wide...one hundred yards deep...and..." he paused, shaking his head in disbelief, "four miles long."

Jon did the multiplication in his journal. "That's—that's—60 million cubic yards of krill?!" More than enough to fill twenty football stadiums.

"There's something else heading our way," Captain Thorn announced. "I'm going to back up. Give us some room." The sub pulled back to the edge of the school of swarming crustaceans.

The sonar pinged wildly. Whatever was coming was big!

Then Jon saw it. An enormous shadow-shape swimming through the krill.

No one in the small cabin said a word as it approached. It was close enough that the tiny submarine rocked with the powerful surging of its huge tail flukes. Jon could see its cavernous mouth opening and closing, taking in monstrous gulps of the tiny shrimp-size creatures that were its only food.

Time seemed to stand still. All that existed was the amazing scene outside the bubble window.

The never-ending school of krill.

And the wondrous blue whale.

Jon knew no matter how long he lived, no matter where he traveled, no matter what else he saw, he would never forget this.

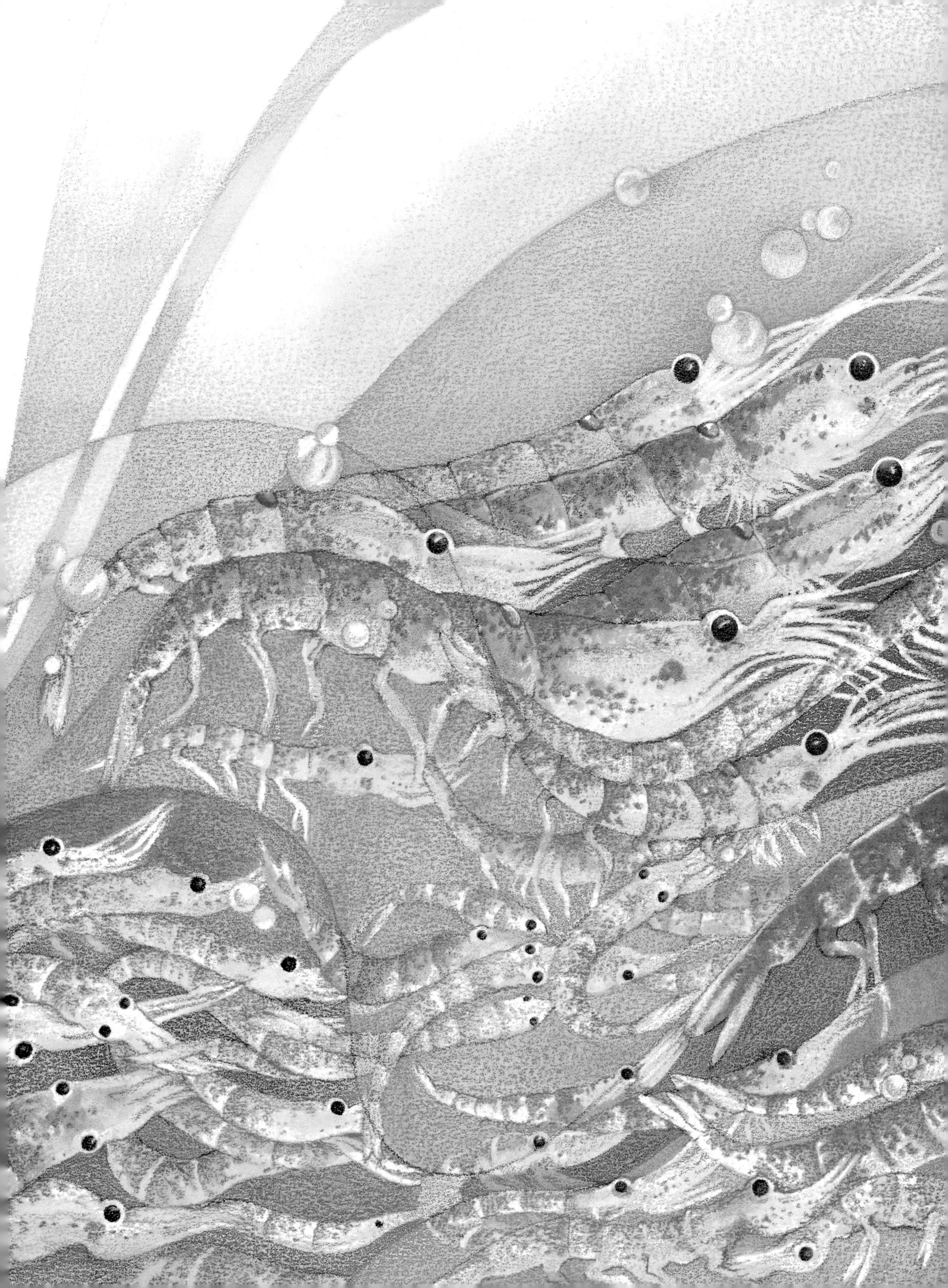

October 17
102 degrees west, 71 degrees south.
Amundsen Sea. 15:00 hours. Temperature 12°F.
Windspeed: 20 mph. Left the peninsula a
couple of days ago. Next stop McMurdo Station.
It's too cold and windy to go out on deck, so Mom
gave me a book about the exploration of
Antarctica. I thought life was tough in the Old
West, but those guys had it easy.

In 1911 two men battled each other, and the worst that Antarctica could set against them, to be the first to stand at the South Pole. The story of their race is one of the greatest adventures in polar exploration. Strangely, the loser of the race is the man history best remembers.

The winner was explorer Roald Amundsen from Norway. His life's dream was to be the first man at the North Pole. But Robert Peary beat him to that on April 6, 1909. So Amundsen turned his dreams of discovery south.

He anchored his ship, the *Fram*, in the Bay of Whales off the Ross Ice Shelf. On Friday, September 8, 1911, he and seven other men set off, along with eighty-six sled dogs pulling six sledges packed with supplies.

Englishman Robert Falcon Scott was already world famous for leading a scientific expedition to Antarctica in 1902. When Scott heard that Amundsen was planning to try for the pole, he was determined to get there first. On October 24, 1911, he and his companions set off for the pole, knowing Amundsen had a head start.

Amundsen's route was shorter and easier than Scott's. But in Antarctica nothing is easy. Battling temperatures often fifty degrees or more below freezing and icy winds blowing more than fifty miles an hour, with frostbitten feet and compasses too frozen to work, the men fought their way across the Ross Ice Shelf and up the Axel Heiberg Glacier. As food and supplies were used up, dogs that were no longer needed to pull the sledges were shot and butchered to feed the remaining animals.

Finally, at 3 o'clock on Friday, December 14, 1911, Amundsen's team planted the flag of Norway at the South Pole. They were the first men to reach the bottom of the earth. Amundsen left a letter for Scott, then made the long trip back to the Bay of Whales.

Scott started off using dogs, motor-sledges and ponies. Overcome by the blizzards and thick snow, the ponies died before the expedition started climbing the Beardmore Glacier at the edge of the ice shelf. The sledges couldn't make it up the steep ice and turned back, along with the dog teams. Scott and eleven men hauled three heavy sledges up the glacier by hand. At the top all but five turned back. Scott, along with Bill Wilson, Lawrence Oates, Henry Bowers and Edgar Evans continued south, carrying all their supplies on their backs.

On January 16, 1912, after sighting one of Amundsen's marker flags, Scott wrote in his diary, "The worst has happened. The Norwegians are first at the Pole.... All dreams must go." Reaching the South Pole the next day, Scott saw the flag Amundsen had left behind. He wrote, "Now for the run home and a desperate struggle. I wonder if we can do it."

It was a terrible journey made in freezing blizzards. Evans died at the edge of the ice shelf. Oates wandered out of camp in a howling blizzard and was never seen again. Scott, Wilson and Bowers kept on as long as they could. But on March 29, Scott made his last journal entry. "...It seems a pity, but I do not think I can write more."

Eight months later a search party found their frozen bodies just eleven miles from a supply camp and safety.

Jon put the book down and tried to imagine how awful that expedition must have been. Outside his comfortable cabin the wind had died down. He got warmly dressed and went up on deck. Giant icebergs sailed slowly by. Birds soared overhead. Seals and penguins hunted around the pack ice. Alone on deck the boy wondered if there was a more beautiful, or more dangerous place anywhere else on earth.

October 27
166 degrees, 30 minutes east, 78 degrees south. McMurdo Sound. 13:30 hours.
Temperature: 10°F. Wind speed: 10 mph.
Unless you count Mary Elizabeth Fleemer in the first grade, I've never been proposed to before today.

The snowmobile churned its way across the thick ice of McMurdo Sound. Behind them was the jumble of low-lying buildings that made up McMurdo Station, the United States' largest research base in Antarctica. Beyond the base rose Mt. Erebus, an active volcano. A plume of smoke trailed from the top of its cone like a flag in the wind.

Jon was driving, careful to follow his mother's directions. She pointed to a low, snow-dotted hillside, and as they got closer Jon could see thousands of penguins dotting the slope.

He stopped several hundred feet away from the rookery, and they got out to walk closer. As they approached, a few of the penguins honked a little nervously, but otherwise they seemed unafraid of the two humans. With their smooth black-and-white feathers patterned like formal jackets, Jon was reminded of guests at a fancy party. He wrinkled his nose. A smelly party, he thought. Penguins were almost as bad as elephant seals!

Many of the birds seemed to be standing around while others waddled busily here and there, heads pointed toward the ground, as though looking for something. Then Jon noticed one penguin carrying a small stone in its beak. It walked up to another standing close by and carefully placed the stone on the ground near its feet.

"What's he doing, Mom?"

"Giving her stones to build their nest. It's part of their courtship and mating ritual. While the male gathers the stones, the female stands guard so their neighbors don't steal them."

As Jon watched, another penguin awkwardly leaned over to pick up a rock. Straightening, it looked around and fastened its gaze on Jon. Then it waddled over to him and dropped the pebble at his feet.

The boy looked down at the bird.

The bird looked up at the boy.

Jon lifted his hands in question. "Okay, Mom. Now what?"

The penguin cocked its head, as though saying, "What are you waiting for? Start building!"

Dr. Michaels laughed. "Either you're standing right where he wants to build his nest, or he wants to mate with you!"

"Come on, Mom!" Jon said, a little embarrassed. Then, realizing how funny it was, they both laughed out loud.

A few minutes later, Jon noticed a small group of penguins several hundred yards out on the ice. "What are they doing?"

"Fishing, I think. Let's get a closer look."

The group of about twenty birds was gathered around a hole in the ice. One at a time they popped out of the water, like corks out of a bottle, while others dived in. Jon was fascinated. As clumsy and awkward as penguins were on land, they were graceful and powerful swimmers, completely at home in the water.

"I don't want you to get any closer, Jon. The ice around that hole looks pretty thin. Besides, we should be getting back soon. The dive starts at six." They were planning to scuba dive under the ice with some scientists from the laboratory at McMurdo.

Jon waved okay and turned back to the birds, but something had changed. Now they seemed nervous. They began honking loudly and flapping their wings. Some ran and belly flopped on the ice, scooting away from the water. Almost as though they were running away from something. Jon stopped, puzzled.

"Jon," his mother called. "You're out too far—"

The water seemed to explode as the head of a killer whale erupted right through the thin ice in front of him. The penguins squawked, scattering in terror. Jon stood frozen to the spot, too frightened to move, as the huge animal turned toward him. It opened its four-foot mouth and he could see rows of long, glistening, razor-edged teeth. With a mighty surge the whale heaved half of its twenty-five-foot-long body out of the water, crashing heavily down onto the ice. What was it trying to do?

Jon heard the cracks before he saw them.

"Run, Jon! Back this way!" his mother yelled. Finally realizing the danger, he quickly turned and leaped across the widening crack in the ice under his feet. His heavy boots slipped as he landed and he fell awkwardly, sliding another ten feet. He scrambled up and looked back to see the block of ice he'd been standing on slowly tilt up under the killer whale's tremendous weight. Jon realized the creature was tilting the ice to spill the penguins into the water! The birds who hadn't made it to safety began sliding helplessly toward the whale's gaping mouth. The sea foamed as the animal twisted and turned. The whale's mouth opened and closed with a terrible swiftness as it made a quick meal of the hapless penguins.

Her arm protectively around her son, Dr. Michaels breathed in relief. "That was a little too close." All Jon could do was nod. His breath came in quick, nervous gasps that turned to white vapor in the chill air.

Soon the patch of water was calm again. The whale was gone, the surviving penguins had scattered far and wide. But in his mind, Jon could see every moment of the violent and sudden attack. And he remembered once again that, as beautiful as it was, Antarctica seldom allowed more than one mistake.

There's this huge drill, about three feet across that makes a hole in the ice big enough for a diver to get through. Then you put a hut over the hole, turn on the heater, and presto! An instant diving platform through eight feet of ice. What was I doing jumping into water that's below freezing?

The ice of McMurdo Sound was a distant, dark blue ceiling overhead. Below and around them was blackness, dark as pockets. Then the divers switched on their lights.

To Jon, who had done his share of diving in tropical reefs, this was yet another world. First of all, since there are no beaches at McMurdo, there was almost no sand. Instead, the bottom was a solid carpet of rocks, coral and giant sponges, some more than six feet tall and shaped like volcanoes.

Jon was also surprised by the brilliant colors that burst out of the darkness—red, orange, yellow, green. And the icy water teemed with life. Veiled and tendriled jellyfish, like delicate, living curtains, slowly moved along, feeding by sifting tiny organisms from the water. Bright orange sea spiders, with spindly legs more than eight inches long, crawled across outcroppings of rock. Starfish and sea anemones, bigger than any Jon had ever seen, were everywhere. The water was several degrees below freezing, yet there were plenty of fish. What protected them?

Later, one of the marine biologists explained that many Antarctic fish have a kind of biological "antifreeze" in their blood. Scientists have been studying this unique evolutionary trick hoping it may lead to the invention of new ways of protecting people in conditions of extreme cold.

Suddenly a dark shape darted into the beams of light. They had drawn the curious attention of a sleek Weddell seal. It spent a long time following them around, perhaps hoping one of the divers would scare up a meal for it. Jon was surprised at how long it stayed under without having to surface for air.

Back at the station his mother told him, "They can dive over 2,000 feet deep and stay under for an hour or more at a time. In winter they live in the water under the ice because it's warmer than the air."

"But they have to come out to breathe!"

"They keep breathing holes open by chewing the ice."

Jon was amazed at the many strange and beautiful creatures that managed to live in the freezing waters of McMurdo Sound.

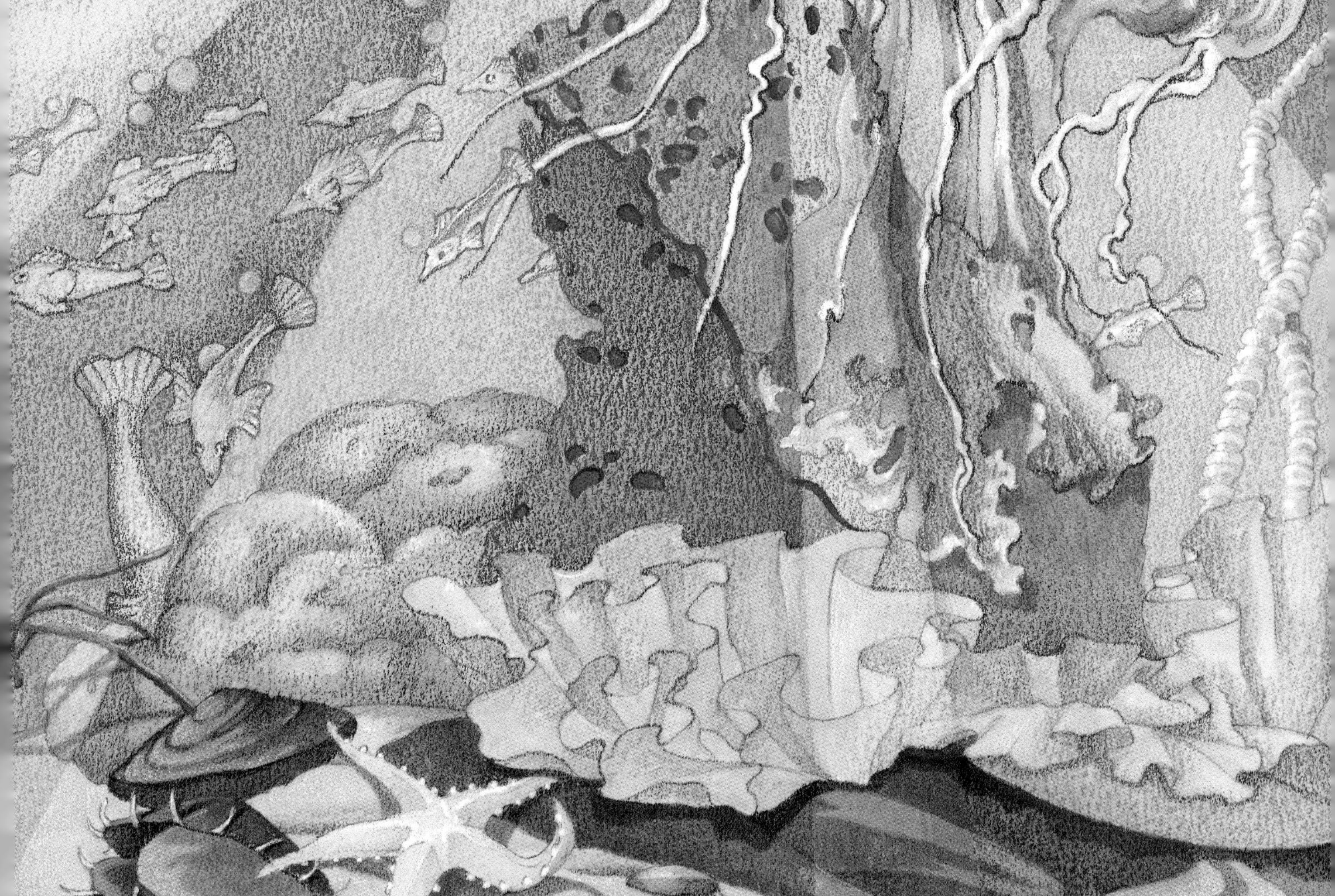

November 7
170 degrees east, 85 degrees south. Over the Beardmore Glacier. 11:00 hours.
We're heading to the South Pole. Sorry if this is hard to read. It's kind of a bumpy ride. They didn't build these planes for comfort, but the view is something else.

The *Hercules* LC-130 roared down the skiway and lifted off from Williams Field, the landing strip built on the permanent ice of the Ross Ice Shelf. Ross Island lay below, its back against the massive sheet of ice.

"Mom, was Antarctica always frozen?"

"Not always. Millions of years ago it was a tropical land with swamps and forests and dinosaurs."

"Dinosaurs!?"

"It was a dinosaur fossil, found in 1969, that convinced scientists Antarctica was once connected to Africa, Australia, India and South America as part of a super-continent called Gondwanaland. In one of the dry mountain valleys down there, they found fossilized remains of a 220-million-year-old swamp with leaves, seeds and branches from trees."

Below and to the west were the Transantarctic Mountains, their jagged peaks piercing the continental ice sheet like spines on a stegosaur's back. Glaciers filled the high mountain valleys and flowed down the passes, spilling out onto the edge of the ice shelf. And, for the first time, Jon began to get a true picture of one of the most incredible structures on the face of the earth.

The Ross Ice Shelf rises straight up from over 850 feet beneath the Ross Sea to over 150 feet above it. Where it joins the Antarctic land mass 650 miles from Ross Island, it averages over 2000 feet thick. "Think of it as a floating ice cube the size of France," Dr. Michaels said. It seemed to go on forever. It must have seemed that way to Robert Scott too, the boy thought.

They were flying above the route Scott and his men had followed. From the sky the ice looked smooth and flat. But Jon knew that was far from true. Ice and snow blown by the wind and frozen into peaks from six inches to six feet tall covered much of the shelf and could make travel almost impossible.

Crevasses were another hazard. The ice shelf was constantly moving—as much as 1000 feet a year. As the ice moved it fractured, forming cracks sometimes hundreds of feet deep. Falling snow often covers these cracks, camouflaging them and making them appear solid. Sleds, dogs, ponies, snowmobiles, trucks and many an unlucky Antarctic traveler have fallen through the snow bridges and been swallowed by the treacherous caverns below.

They passed beyond Beardmore Glacier and the Transantarctic Mountains and came to a plateau of ice. Mile after endless mile. Flat and featureless. Built up inch by inch, year after year, for millions upon millions of years. An icy blanket, over two miles thick, that stretched across the broad back of the continent.

The flight promised to be smooth and easy the rest of the way; in another hour or two they would be at the South Pole. Jon settled back in the seat harness, ready to catch up on his journal, but before writing more than a few lines, he got a frightening reminder that, in Antarctica, nothing is easy.

The plane's radio crackled to life. "Hercules *Alpha Foxtrot two-three-six, this is Amundsen-Scott Base. Be advised ground conditions here are going bad fast. Visibility two miles. Wind 60 knots and rising. What's your estimated time of arrival?*"

"ETA 1330 hours," the pilot answered.

"That's cutting it close. We'll have landing strobes lit and emergency vehicles on standby."

Outside the window the sky was a pale white ceiling. "Uh, Mom, what do you call it when you can't tell the sky from the ground?"

"Oh, no," she whispered. "A white-out."

A white-out is one of the most frightening weather conditions in the Antarctic. The snow-covered ground merges with the snow-white clouds until you can't tell where one stops and the other starts. Birds, confused by the loss of reference points, fly right into the ground; men wander, completely lost, unable to tell one direction from another, until they freeze to death.

Racing headlong toward a blizzard, through a world so featureless they might as well have been flying in a cotton ball, Jon had never felt so completely helpless. The last thirty minutes of the flight were the longest in his life. He couldn't imagine any plane could take so much punishment. It bucked, pitched and plunged like a rodeo bull; the wind hammered at the fuselage like fists. There was nothing to do but go on and try to land at the pole. They couldn't turn back—not enough fuel. They couldn't land anywhere else—there are no alternate airports in Antarctica. It was do or die. And for a few minutes no one knew which it would be.

In the end it was the ruggedness of the LC-130, the reliability of its instruments and the incredible flying skill of the pilot and copilot that made the difference.

When they touched down on the ice at the South Pole everyone on board broke into cheers. The pilot wiped the sweat off his forehead and smiled grimly. "It's not over yet," he said.

They soon found out what he meant.

Everyone pulled on parkas, ski masks and goggles and stood, waiting to get off. When the door finally opened, Jon was nearly thrown off his feet by the force of the wind. And the cold was like nothing he'd ever felt before. Even through the mask it was like tiny needles in his skin.

They wore safety lines as they fought their way across the ice to the trucks waiting to take them to the base. Jon was grateful the others knew where they were going because he couldn't see a thing. The footing was next to impossible. In that short distance he was blown off his feet half a dozen times and had to be helped up. Without the line he would have been blown away. And in this weather, that's the last anyone would have seen of him. Alive, anyway.

The trucks had massive tank-treads for traction on the ice. The powerful engines started up, and they slowly made their way to the station. When they stopped, Jon climbed out and looked around. They were inside a large geodesic dome built to cover many smaller buildings, fuel storage bladders, heating, snow-melting and research equipment. The temperature was only slightly warmer in here, but at least they weren't being whipped by those terrible winds.

What a welcome to the South Pole!

November 10
0 degrees longitude, 90 degrees south. Amundsen-Scott Station, South Pole. 10:15 hours. Temperature -40°F. Wind speed: 140 mph. I don't think this wind's ever going to stop. At least there's plenty to do—a gym, movie theater, good food, scientists from all over the world to talk to. . . .

The blizzard lasted three days. On the morning of the fourth, Jon woke up with the feeling something was different. It took him a minute to realize what it was. Of course! The wind had stopped! He hurriedly dressed and joined his mother for breakfast.

"Are you ready?" she asked after they finished.

"Ready? Are you kidding? Let's go!"

They pulled their parkas on and went outside. It was a beautiful day, though it was still a numbing -26°F. Jon turned around, grinning when he realized that no matter which way he looked he was facing north. Flags were flying from the big dome and many of the other buildings. Radio antennas and radar dishes dotted the landscape. People in brightly colored parkas were moving around, on their way from one area to another, one experiment to the next. All in all, it was a picture of busy, purposeful activity.

"Where is it?" Jon asked, looking around.

"Right over there."

A short pole with a shiny dome surrounded by flags stood a few hundred feet away. The real South Pole! He'd made it! Jon took off running.

When he reached the pole, he was grinning and out of breath. He had dreamed about what he would do when he finally got here. Now he closed his eyes and pictured a globe in his mind, seeing all the lines of longitude arching out from the North Pole like slices of a pie, spreading apart at the equator, then curving to meet again at a single imaginary point right where he was standing at the South Pole.

He pictured where 76 degrees west longitude was, then, lifting his foot and taking a step, he said, "Washington, D.C." East, a hop, skip and jump across the Atlantic Ocean, was 0 degrees and "London!" Another step east to 37 degrees brought him to "Moscow!" Next, straddling the entire continent of Asia and feeling like Godzilla, he put his foot down at about 139 degrees and stepped on "Tokyo!" Then, with one final bound, he leapfrogged the Pacific Ocean and landed at 118 degrees west, completing his circle around the pole. "California!" he shouted triumphantly.

He looked up to see his mother focusing the camera, ready to take his picture. He waved and shouted, "Wow! What a trip! I just walked around the world!"

I'm about two miles from the station right now. Mom's taking some deep-ice samples nearby. If Captain Thorn were here, he'd probably call this "a nice day." Blue sky, light wind, temperature about -30°F. Know what? It is a nice day!

We'll be flying home tomorrow by way of McMurdo Station, then Christchurch, New Zealand, and Honolulu. The Captain's staying at McMurdo with MURV for another couple of weeks. I have a lot of schoolwork to make up, but Mom wants to take a few days for some sightseeing in Hawaii before we head back to the mainland. Sounds great, only there's no ice in Hawaii! That sounds funny, I guess, but maybe Antarctica's spoiled me. It's all those things Mom told me: the highest, coldest, windiest, driest. But she left out some other things: the most beautiful, the loneliest, the most dangerous. . . .

And the quietest. I'm standing at the bottom of the world and there's almost nothing around for thousands of miles. It's like I can hear forever.